PUFFIN BOOKS

Pirate Pandemonium

Jeremy Strong once worked in a bakery, putting the jam into 3,000 doughnuts every night. Now he puts the jam in stories instead, which he finds much more exciting. At the age of three he fell out of a first-floor bedroom window and landed on his head. His mother says that this damaged him for the rest of his life and refuses to take any responsibility. He loves writing stories because he says it is 'the only time you alone have complete control and can make anything happen'. His ambition is to make you laugh (or at least snuffle). Jeremy Strong lives in Kent with his wife, Susan, two cats, and a pheasant that sits on the garden fence with a 'can't catch me' grin on his beak.

Other books by Jeremy Strong

THE AIR-RAID SHELTER
THE DESPERATE ADVENTURES OF SIR RUPERT
AND ROSIE GUSSET
DINOSAUR POX
FANNY WITCH AND THE THUNDER LIZARD
FANNY WITCH AND THE WICKED WIZARD
FATBAG: THE DEMON VACUUM CLEANER
GIANT JIM AND THE HURRICANE
THE HUNDRED-MILE-AN-HOUR DOG
THE INDOOR PIRATES

THE KARATE PRINCESS
THE KARATE PRINCESS AND THE CUT-THROAT
ROBBERS
THE KARATE PRINCESS TO THE RESCUE
THE KARATE PRINCESS AND THE LAST GRIFFIN

LIGHTNING LUCY
MY DAD'S GOT AN ALLIGATOR!
MY GRANNY'S GREAT ESCAPE
PANDEMONIUM AT SCHOOL
THERE'S A PHARAOH IN OUR BATH
THERE'S A VIKING IN MY BED
VIKING AT SCHOOL
VIKING IN TROUBLE

Jeremy Strong

Pirate Pandemonium

Illustrated by Judy Brown

PUFFIN BOOKS

For Jane, and arnarchy and imagination
in the classroom

PUFFIN BOOKS

Published by the Penguin Group
Penguin Books Ltd, 27 Wrights Lane, London W8 5TZ, England
Penguin Putnam Inc., 375 Hudson Street, New York, New York 10014, USA
Penguin Books Australia Ltd, Ringwood, Victoria, Australia
Penguin Books Canada Ltd, 10 Alcorn Avenue, Toronto, Ontario, Canada M4V 3B2
Penguin Books (NZ) Ltd, Private Bag 102902, NSMC, Auckland, New Zealand

On the World Wide Web at: www.penguin.com

Penguin Books Ltd, Registered Offices: Harmondsworth, Middlesex, England

First published by A & C Black (Publishers) Ltd 1997
Published in Puffin Books 1999
1 3 5 7 9 10 8 6 4 2

Text copyright © Jeremy Strong, 1997
Illustrations copyright © Judy Brown, 1997
All rights reserved

The moral right of the author and illustrator has been asserted

Filmset in Baskerville MT

Made and printed in England by Clays Ltd, St Ives plc

British Library Cataloguing in Publication Data
A CIP catalogue record for this book is available from the British Library

ISBN 0-141-30493-6

Contents

1 A Telephone Call 1

2 Intoducing Class Five – Beware! 17

3 Battle Commences 37

4 Give Us Your Treasure! 52

5 Tricky Tracey 67

6 Mrs Earwigger's Revenge 84

7 The Pirates Go Kidnapping 99

1 A Telephone Call

It was a rather strange shape. It was meant to be a clay elephant, but it looked more like the result of a high-speed, head-on collision between an octopus and a hippopotamus. Violet Pandemonium had only recently taken up pottery. She had been getting rather bored and needed something to do. Normally she had plenty of work as a supply teacher, but recently not a single school had telephoned her to ask if she would like to come and look after a class because the teacher was ill. Miss Pandemonium could not understand it. 'Perhaps the government has banned teachers from being ill,' she wondered.

Then one day she noticed in the local

newspaper that someone was selling:

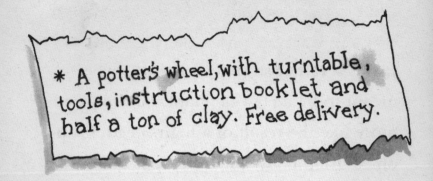

* A potter's wheel, with turntable, tools, instruction booklet and half a ton of clay. Free delivery.

Miss Pandemonium thought it sounded like a chance not to be missed. 'I've always fancied going potty,' she giggled, and rang up immediately and bought the lot.

Violet had not realized how much half a ton of clay was. She lived in a small house in the middle of a terrace, with no front garden and, being rather short of space, she had to put the clay in her bath, where it sat like some hideous misshapen life-form. Excitedly, she set up the potter's wheel at once, put her foot on the treadle and soon had the wheel spinning round at a fine rate. She grabbed a nice big blob of clay and stuck it on the wheel. Much to her surprise the clay was immediately flung off at high speed. Violet watched as it whizzed across the room and splattered across Auntie Dora's face. Fortunately it was only a photograph of Auntie Dora.

Miss P. cleaned up Auntie as best she could, blew her a kiss by way of an apology and had another try. The second blob of clay did much the same thing, except that it flew off in a different direction, zoomed out through the open window and hit a passing cyclist. It flopped over his head like a big brown pancake.

Unable to see where he was going, the cyclist rode straight up a plank and into the back of a builder's van. When the builder went to his van to get some bricks he found a dazed cyclist with something like a cowpat sitting on his head, trying to untangle himself from the remains of his twisted bike.

As for Violet Pandemonium, she had no idea what had happened. She was still searching round her front room, wondering where the clay missile had gone. The potter's wheel was proving to be a little unpredictable, so Miss P. decided to try some modelling with her hands instead. That was when she made the elephant – or was it a hippopoctopus?

She was just putting the finishing touches to it when the telephone rang. Miss Pandemonium jumped up to answer it. 'Hello . . . yes, I'm Miss Pandemonium, at least I was when I got up this morning . . . oh! . . . straight away? Well yes, I can. Which school is it? Witts End Primary . . . a class of nine- and ten-year-olds . . . yes, that's fine . . . I shall be with you in half an hour . . . bye-eee!'

Miss P. tried to put the phone down, but her hands were covered in wet clay and the telephone stuck to her as if it had been glued to her fingers. She pulled the phone from her right hand with her left and the phone stuck to her left hand instead. After several minutes, she eventually managed to escape by pushing the phone out of her hand with one elbow. She had clay halfway up both arms, and the phone was now attached to her left elbow. She shook it off, rushed to the kitchen, had a good wash and then set about getting ready for school.

Miss Pandemonium quickly stuffed a multitude of bits and bobs into a big canvas holdall. 'Now, let's see, have I got everything? Have I got my bag of teaching gear? Yes. Have I got my lunch? No. I shall have to have a school lunch today. Have I got my First Aid bag, my

Medical Encyclopaedia and Emergency Acupuncture Kit? Yes. Have I got my glasses? No – don't be silly, Violet, you don't wear glasses. OK, let's go!'

Miss Pandemonium rushed out through the front door, dropped a bag, picked it up, leapt into her second-hand ambulance and set off for Witts End Primary School with all lights flashing and the siren wailing.

It was astonishing how empty the roads were when Miss Pandemonium went out in her ambulance. Cars hastily pulled over to one side. Lorries stopped dead. Even the police cheerily waved her on, thinking there was a major emergency somewhere. Miss P. had a clear and easy drive to the school. With a haul on the steering wheel she skidded into the Witts Ends School car park, siren still blaring, found a parking space, did a five-point turn with gears

crunching, screeched to a halt and jumped
out.

'Oh!' said Miss Pandemonium as she
turned to go into the school. 'A welcoming
committee – how nice!' Peering from every
window were faces – children's faces,
teachers' faces, cooks' faces, the secretary,
the caretaker, and the head teacher.
Everyone had heard the siren. Everyone

had seen the ambulance arrive. Now they could all see Miss Pandemonium too.

Mr Kuddle, the head teacher, hurried across the car park to meet her, stooping to pick up her bags as she dropped them one by one. 'So glad you're here,' he began, retrieving bag number one. 'I'm Mr Kuddle. I'm the head. You can call me Kevin – everybody does – well, to my face anyway, ha ha! Who knows what they call me behind my back! Ha ha! Lovely ambulance – lovely. Mrs Colon – she has Class Five usually – she's got a bit of a tummy problem and won't be back for two weeks or so. Nice class, Class Five – got some characters in there, I can tell you, ha ha! Be firm but kind, that's what I say. We must earn their respect. That's Class Five over there, the ones that are waving and shouting at us – oh look, I think Samantha

Boggis has just thrown Gary out of the window. Never mind, he's used to it. He knows his way back. Lovely girl, Samantha – bags of character. Well, good luck, Miss um, Miss um-mum . . .?'

'Pandemonium,' smiled Miss P., who was at last able to get a word in. 'But call me Violet.'

'Kevin,' nodded Mr Kuddle.

Miss Pandemonium frowned slightly.

'No, not Kevin, Violet.'

Now Mr

Kuddle seemed confused. 'I'm not Violet,' he said.

'No, I am,' said Miss Pandemonium. 'That's my name.

Why did you call me Kevin?'

'Did I? How odd. Kevin is my name.'

They both stopped by the main entrance. 'So I'm Kevin and you're Violet,' repeated Mr Kuddle, and his bushy moustache gave a cheerful wriggle. 'Good, ha ha! Class Five is up the corridor, last door on the left. Lovely children, lovely. High-spirited little lot! We have a busy time ahead – it's Book Week, you know, and we are having a new school library opened on Friday by the Mayor. Each class is choosing a special book topic and everybody's going to dress up. Thought I'd come as Robocop, ha ha! Oh well, see you later um, Violin.'

Before Miss Pandemonium could correct him, he had gone scurrying back to his little office and shutting the door quickly behind him. Miss Pandemonium

grasped her bags
firmly and set off
down the long
corridor.

Halfway down the
corridor a classroom
door suddenly flew
open and a striking
figure appeared. A
tall, thin, elderly lady
stood framed in the
doorway. She was
wearing what
looked like a long
black evening
dress, and she

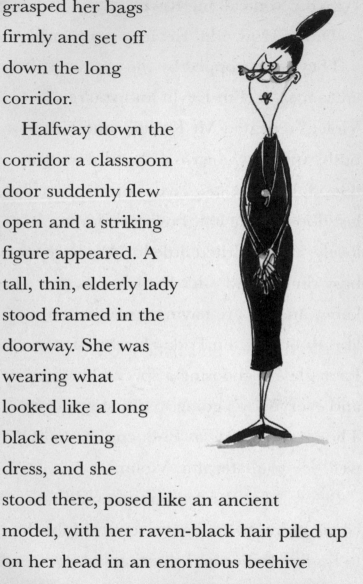

stood there, posed like an ancient
model, with her raven-black hair piled up
on her head in an enormous beehive
hairdo. She whipped off her vulture-like

glasses and fixed Violet with a penetrating glare.

'Mrs Earwigger,' she announced curtly. 'Deputy head. You're in the room next door. No noise. Thank you.' And with that she gave a brief nod and vanished back into her classroom.

Violet Pandemonium put down her bags and stared in surprise at the shut door. She went across to it, pulled the door open, poked her cheerful face round the frame and smiled in at Mrs Earwigger, who appeared most shocked that anyone had opened her door at all, especially without knocking. After all, nobody ever dared to go anywhere near her room.

A sea of curious little faces gazed back at Miss Pandemonium. A visitor! They never had visitors! Visitors to Mrs Earwigger's class were like aliens from a distant planet.

Violet smiled across at the astonished
deputy head.

'Violet Pandemonium,' she announced.
'Supply teacher. I'm in the class next door.
Loads of noise. I've come to teach them
how to tap dance and play the drums.
Bye-eee.' And with that she closed the
door, picked up her bags and went.

Inside Mrs Earwigger's classroom you
could have heard a pin drop. Mrs
Earwigger stared at the classroom door as

if it had just stuck out its tongue at her and burped, very loudly. The children stared at Mrs Earwigger, wondering what she would do next, glancing at each other, with tiny smiles hiding on their lips.

Then Mrs Earwigger's mouth began to do something very strange. The children didn't find it strange at all, because Mrs Earwigger's mouth was famous for doing exactly this. In fact, the children often tried to copy it in the playground, but nobody did it as well as Mrs Earwigger herself.

Her mouth began to scrunch up. It sucked itself inwards, so that her thin lips puckered up into a mass of wrinkles, and finally her mouth disappeared, just as if she had swallowed it. This is what Mrs Earwigger did when she was totally flabbergasted. Other people might shout, scream, pull their hair and jump up and down, but Mrs Earwigger sucked up her mouth until it vanished.

Miss Pandemonium had arrived, and nothing and nobody at Witts End Primary School would ever be quite the same.

2 Introducing Class Five – Beware!

Miss Pandemonium pushed open the door of Class Five and walked in. She was used to being greeted by a huddle of children with expectant faces, sitting quietly at their tables. But Class Five was different. They were not in a huddle, they were not quiet and they were not looking the least bit expectant either.

Samantha Boggis was busy throwing Gary out of a window for the fifth time that morning. A large group of children at the back of the class appeared to be having an 'Everybody-Welcome-to-Wrestling' competition. And a section of Samantha Boggis's all-girl gang had captured three boys and sentenced them to a life of slavery.

'Good morning, everyone!' cried Miss Pandemonium cheerfully. She was completely ignored. Violet watched them for a few moments. 'I see,' she muttered to herself, and dived into her enormous hold-all. First of all she pulled out a small, portable electric cooker, put it on her desk and plugged it into a wall socket. Then she went back to the bag and got out a large empty tin can, with a screw top.

The bunch of wrestlers stopped tying each other into knots and sat down to watch the strange woman doing even stranger things with a tin can. Violet took the empty can to the sink and poured a little cold water into it. Then she took the can back to her desk and placed it on the cooker. While the water was coming to the boil Violet set about cleaning the blackboard, which was covered with remarks like:

'Tom Nunnery stinks'

'Tracey loves Mike'

'Darren Oates has pimples on his b —'

(The rest was smeared.)

Miss Pandemonium appeared to completely ignore the children, most of whom had now slipped quietly back to their tables and had their eyes glued to the tin can on the cooker. Steam was spouting up from the little hole in the top.

'It's boiling, miss,' said Darren.

'Oh! So it is.' Miss Pandemonium turned from the clean blackboard, switched off the cooker and removed the can from the heat. She picked up the screw top and carefully screwed the lid on to the can. Then she put it on her desk and without a word began to unpack some of her bits and pieces. Even Samantha Boggis and her gang now had their eyes fixed on the can. What on earth was this weird woman doing?

Nothing happened, and then, just as Class Five were beginning to get restless

once again, there was a
loud CLUNK, and
one wall of the tin
can bent inwards.

This was quickly
followed by another
loud CLANG, and
the whole tin doubled
over, as if it had been

punched in the belly by a gigantic
invisible fist.

There was one more ear-splitting
SCRANG, and the tin completely
collapsed in upon
itself, toppled
over and crashed
to the floor.

Class Five rose to
their feet and stared down at

the crumpled can. Then they looked at each other with bewildered faces. 'How did that happen?' demanded Samantha. 'How did you do that?'

'Air pressure,' answered Miss Pandemonium. 'Steam drove the air from the can, so that when I put the lid on there was less air inside the can than there was outside it. That meant there was more air pressure outside than there was inside, so the can was crushed by air pressure.'

'Do it again!' cried Mike.

'Bring me a can tomorrow and I'll do it again,' smiled Violet. Tracey frowned.

'Are you here tomorrow then?'

'Yes. I'm here until Mrs Colon gets better.'

'That's what Mrs Earwigger does,' a voice said quietly from the back of the class. Everyone turned round and glared at a small, freckled boy.

'Oh shut up, Gary!' they cried.

'But she does,' insisted Gary. 'It must be air pressure. When she gets all cross and steamy she shuts her mouth and then it all sucks in on itself, just like that tin can. I bet it's air pressure.'

'Gary,' said Samantha threateningly, 'if you open your mouth once more I'm going to stuff your plimsoll bag inside it.'

'Oh, I don't think so,' said Mrs Pandemonium. 'We have far more important things to do. I hear it's Book Week this week, and everybody is going to dress up. Mr Kuddle told me that each class is choosing a special topic. Have you chosen one yet?'

After several grunts and grumbles Michelle explained that nobody was ever allowed to choose a theme for Book Week because Mrs Earwigger always decided what everyone was going to do.

'I see,' murmured Miss Pandemonium. 'Mrs Earwigger decides what every class will do, not just her own class?' The children nodded glumly. 'What would happen if we chose a topic for ourselves?' asked Violet.

Eyes began to boggle. Jaws dropped. Eyebrows shot all over the place, and there

was a severe outbreak of spine-chilling goosepimples.

There was such an air of excited, scared astonishment that Miss Pandemonium got the impression that such a thing had never been heard of before. She asked the class if Mrs Earwigger had chosen a topic for Class Five yet.

'Yes,' said Ryan. 'Flower Fairies. Mrs Earwigger has got a Flower Fairies Address Book, and it's her most favourite book and she wants everyone in Class Five to dress up as a Flower Fairy.' For some reason Ryan didn't sound too enthusiastic about the idea.

'Yes, that sounds very interesting,' said Miss Pandemonium, who wasn't at all sure that Book Weeks were meant to celebrate address books. 'And are you all looking forward to being Flower Fairies?'

This question produced an explosion of answers. 'In that case,' said Miss Pandemonium, 'we had better think of something else. How about Winnie-the-Pooh?'

'Winnie-the-Pooh stinks,' muttered Tony, much to everyone's amusement.

'Robinson Crusoe?' Miss Pandemonium offered.

'There's only one Robinson Crusoe,' Cleo pointed out. 'We can't all be Robinson Crusoe.'

'Very true,' murmured Miss P. 'All right, what about Peter Pan?'

'There are fairies in Peter Pan,' grumbled James, 'and loads of goody-goodies.'

'Yeah, but there's Captain Hook and his pirates,' said Samantha. 'I could be Captain Hook.'

'You're a girl!' yelled Darren. 'Girls can't be pirate captains!'

'Who says!' screeched Samantha, jumping to her feet and fixing Darren with a murderous stare.

'Why don't we all be pirates?' said Miss Pandemonium calmly. 'We don't have to do Peter Pan at all. We can do a class topic on pirates and then everyone can be a pirate.'

This last suggestion seemed to go down pretty well, until Tom said that girls couldn't be pirates because girls were too girly and didn't know how to hold a sword properly and could never kill anyone because they'd be too busy wanting to be nurses instead. 'They'd stick their sword in someone and then say, "Oh, terribly sorry, have I made you bleed? Here, let me bandage it up for you".'

The boys roared with laughter, until Samantha stood on her chair and glared at them furiously. 'I bet girls make much better pirates than boys,' she shouted, daring the boys to say otherwise. Darren and Wayne needed no encouragement. They leapt from their tables, brandishing their rulers fiercely. 'Come on then, prove it!' they challenged. Within seconds there was a full-scale battle between the boys on one side and the girls on the other. Rulers flashed in the sunlight, fierce faces growled and gnashed their teeth, while Miss Pandemonium seized a metre ruler and stood on her desk, urging the girls on to victory, waving her metre-sword round her head and bashing the light fittings several times as she did so.

'Charge!' screamed Samantha, hurling herself across the classroom.

'Stand by to repel boarders!' roared Mike.

Just as the fight reached fever pitch, the door opened and Mrs Earwigger marched straight in, blowing a shrill whistle. Everyone stopped and looked at the deputy head. Mrs Earwigger glared up at Miss Pandemonium.

'What on earth is going on in here?' demanded Mrs Earwigger.

'We were trying to decide if women pirates are better than men pirates,' Miss

Pandemonium explained, as she struggled to replace one of the light fittings she had knocked down. 'I think it was pretty even actually. What do you think, Mrs Earwigger?'

'What do I think? I have never heard anything like it in my life.'

'You've never heard pirates fighting before?' asked Miss Pandemonium.

'No, of course not! I mean, it's ridiculous. And you – you're standing on your desk.'

'Yes?'

'Teachers don't stand on their desks in this school!' snapped the deputy.

'Oh. Why's that?' asked Miss Pandemonium innocently. 'You see, this is the quarterdeck really. I was standing on the quarterdeck to get a better view of my pirate crew.'

'Your pirate crew!'

'Yes. We've decided to be pirates for Book Week. That's our topic.'

'But you can't. You're a Flower Fairy. You're all Flower Fairies.' Mrs Earwigger was beside herself.

'Not any more,' Miss Pandemonium explained. 'We've decided we prefer being pirates, haven't we, children?'

The astonished children nodded dumbly. Mrs Earwigger was totally gobsmacked. She drew in her breath sharply, closed her mouth and began her party trick.

'Air pressure,' hissed Gary. 'You watch.' And everyone did, as Mrs Earwigger's mouth crumpled up and all of a sudden vanished. The deputy head stalked out of the room and slammed the door shut. There was a sigh of relief from the children and they went back to their chairs.

'You're in trouble now, miss,' said Samantha, with some admiration.

'Why, what have I done?'

'You've changed her Book Week plan. We're going to be pirates and that's going to be much better than what Class Six are going to be. Nobody's supposed to be better than Class Six because it's Mrs Earwigger's class and they're always the best. Nobody has ever changed what Mrs Earwigger says, and you answered back to her.'

'You're not supposed to answer back,' explained Kimberley. 'You're just supposed to listen. Even Mr Kuddle doesn't answer back to Mrs Earwigger.'

'Really? How strange. Tell me, what is Class Six's topic?'

'Roman Gods and Goddesses,' announced Dawn. 'Class Six do Gods and Goddesses every time we dress up for Book Week. They come as Jupiter and Venus and Mars and all that lot. Then they all stand around looking very snooty and they order everyone about.'

'I see,' murmured Miss Pandemonium. 'I must admit that Gods and Goddesses doesn't sound terribly exciting. Well, I think we had better get on with our topic. I guess we have proved that girls can be good pirates too and in fact there used to be quite a lot of famous women pirates that sailed the seven seas.'

'Is that true, miss?' asked Samantha, who was just as amazed to hear this as everyone else.

'Oh yes,' said Miss Pandemonium. 'Several of them ended up walking the plank, just like the men pirates.'

'Can we do walking the plank as well, miss?' asked Wayne. 'I'd like to be in charge of that.'

'Maybe we'll leave that till a bit later. What we need to do first is find out about pirates – how they lived, how they dressed and so on, so that we get some ideas for what we want to wear and what we are going to do.'

There was an immediate rush to the book shelves in the classroom to see what could be discovered about pirates, and Miss Pandemonium settled down to a peaceful morning. As the children started to collect the information they needed Miss Pandemonium turned her thoughts to the deputy head. What a strange woman Mrs Earwigger was, and why did everyone do what she said all the time?

3 Battle Commences

Mrs Earwigger stood in Mr Kuddle's little office glaring down her nose at the head teacher. Mr Kuddle sat hunched at his desk, looking distinctly uncomfortable. It was a big desk and he was very fond of it – when he sat on the far side it was difficult for anyone to get near him, especially Mrs Earwigger. Mr Kuddle spent a lot of his time making sure that there was as much distance between himself and Mrs Earwigger as possible.

'She was standing on her table, Mr Kuddle,' snapped the deputy head. 'The children were fighting and this . . . woman . . . was encouraging them. Now, what are we going to do about it?'

'This is Miss Pandemonium's first day here,' began Mr Kuddle. 'I think we should all be friends. A friendly school is a happy school.'

'Mr Kuddle, Class Five were practising at being pirates,' explained Mrs Earwigger. The head teacher mumbled something about pirates being very appropriate for Class Five, but luckily the deputy didn't hear him. 'What is more,' she continued, 'Class Five are going to be pirates for the whole of Book Week.'

'Good idea.'

'It is not a good idea at all, Mr Kuddle,' snapped Mrs Earwigger. 'If you remember,

I have already decided what everyone will be for our Book Week. Mrs Patel is going to be Snow White and her four-year-olds are going to be the seven dwarfs.'

'But there are twenty-seven children in Mrs Patel's reception class, not seven.'

'I am well aware of that, Mr Kuddle, but they are the only children small enough to be dwarfs,' Mrs Earwigger pointed out with flawless logic.

'Mrs Patel is not exactly, er . . .' Poor Mr Kuddle struggled to find the right words.

'I agree that Mrs Patel is not ideal for Snow White. She is rather large and fifty-three years old, but I'm sure her little dwarfs won't mind.'

Mr Kuddle wasn't so sure about this, but he didn't have the courage to pursue it further. 'What about Class Two?' he sighed.

'Noddy and the Toyland folk,' said his deputy cheerfully, and she carried on with her list. 'Class Three are going to be rabbits.'

'Rabbits? All of them?'

'Yes, you know, Flopsy, Mopsy, Popsy, Wopsy, Topsy, Bopsy, Slopsy, Chopsy . . . all those rabbits that Beatrix Potter wrote about.'

'I'm not sure there was a Popsy,' began Mr Kuddle, 'or a Slopsy, or a Topsy for that matter.'

'There's no point in getting picky about it, Mr Kuddle. Class Three are all going to be rabbits. Besides, we're getting off the point. The reason I am here is because Miss Pandemonium has told Class Five

they can be pirates, and it doesn't fit in
with my Book Week plans at all, so what
are you going to do about it?'

The head teacher tugged nervously at
his big moustache. 'Let's give Miss
Pandemonium a day or two to settle in.
Remember that she has got Class Five,
and they are a difficult bunch.'

'I'm sure I'd have no difficulties with
them,' snapped the deputy.

'No,' agreed Mr Kuddle, thinking that
Mrs Earwigger wouldn't have any
difficulty wrestling Jaws with her bare
hands. 'But Miss Pandemonium has only
just arrived at the school and she is helping
us out until Mrs Colon comes back.' Mr
Kuddle suddenly felt rather brave. 'I say
we let the children be pirates.'

Mrs Earwigger stared at the head
teacher. She couldn't believe her ears. Mr

Kuddle was actually daring to oppose her. He had never opposed her in all the five years that he had been head. It was all that wretched woman's doing: Miss Pandemonium had a lot to answer for. 'You are going to allow Class Five to be pirates?'

Mr Kuddle swallowed hard and nodded, trying to avoid the spear-like glare that Mrs Earwigger had stabbed him with.

'You will let them run riot all over the school, causing mayhem and injury?'

'I don't think it will be like that,' murmured Mr Kuddle, desperately hoping that it wouldn't. 'I'm quite sure that Miss Pandemonium will have everything under control.'

'On your head be it,' snapped the deputy, and she stalked out, slamming the door. Mr Kuddle closed his eyes and began

to plan his next summer holiday.
Would South America be far
enough away?

Mrs Earwigger
stood outside the door
for a moment,
recovering her composure. She
patted her black beehive so that it
stood straight and tall. Her eyes
narrowed until they
were thin,
determined
slits. There was
no way she was
going to have all
her plans changed by
a mere supply teacher like Miss
Pandemonium. Oh no, that woman was in
for a very nasty shock.

*

By the middle of the afternoon, Class Five were deep into pirate lore and had begun collecting ideas for what kind of pirates they wanted to be. Wayne was so taken with having a black eyepatch that he decided he was going to wear two.

'Don't be stupid,' Cleo snorted. 'If you wear two you'll be blind.'

'So? I can be a blind pirate if I want to.' But even Wayne didn't sound too convinced.

'It says here that pirates often kept pets on board ship,' Michelle called out. 'I'm going to be a pirate with a pet.'

'You've only got a stick insect at home,' shouted James. 'How can you be a pirate with a stick insect?'

'Yeah, but my uncle's got a monkey and I'm going to bring that in.'

'Your uncle's never got a monkey!'
James was distinctly jealous.

'Has, so there.'

'Well, he'll never let you bring it in,' said
James, but Michelle just smiled at him and
stuck out her tongue.

'Are you going to be a pirate, miss?'
Darren asked Miss Pandemonium.

'Oh yes. I've already decided who I'm
going to be, I shall be Captain
Blackbeard.'

'Oh! We thought you'd be a woman
pirate.'

'I could be, but I've always fancied being
Blackbeard. He had a long, wild black
hair, and he used to tie gunpowder fuses
into it and light them before he leapt on to
the enemy ship. He must have looked
terrifying.'

'Sounds a bit like Mrs Earwigger,'

muttered Jennifer, and everyone laughed.

'Can we have a boat?' Gary suddenly asked.

'Gary!' the whole class chorused. 'You're so stupid!'

But Miss Pandemonium thought it was an excellent suggestion. 'We can't have a real boat, but why don't we turn this classroom into our pirate galleon? Look, the windows down the side can be our gun-ports . . .'

'Yeah – brilliant! We can make cannons and stick them out of the window and shoot everyone,' cried Stewart.

'And we can make prisoners walk the plank,' hissed Samantha Boggis, looking directly at the hapless Gary. 'I'm going to enjoy this.'

Miss Pandemonium gazed at the sea of happy, interested faces. This was going to

be a lovely week, she thought. Little did
she realize just what Class Five would get
up to – let alone Class Six. Class Six was
the top class, the oldest class, and it was
Mrs Earwigger's class. Nobody
was allowed to teach Year
Six children except Mrs
Earwigger. This could
have been because Mrs
Earwigger didn't like little
children who needed their
laces tying and their noses

wiped; who couldn't hold scissors properly and had a habit of being sick in the sand tray.

It could have been because the youngest children knew the least, so they needed the most teaching. It could also have been because teaching Year Six children was, compared to meeting the demands of the very young, quite an easy life. Or it could have been, as Mrs Earwigger always claimed, that Year Six were the most demanding children who required the finest teaching possible – in other words hers.

Class Six were not looking forward to Book Week. They knew exactly what to expect, and when Mrs Earwigger told them they could all come as Roman Gods and Goddesses they just gazed glumly at each other. She pinned a list next to the blackboard from which the children could choose such delightfully interesting characters as Cupid, Aurora, Mercury and so on.

Class Six were so excited by this that they couldn't even speak and, eventually, when one boy did manage to say something it sounded surprisingly like a groan of despair.

Mrs Earwigger spent the whole lunch hour and half the afternoon with her brain in a whirl. It was as if all the bees in her beehive hairdo had escaped into her brain, and there they buzzed, menacingly. What could she do to outsmart that wretched Miss Pandemonium? If Class Five dressed up as pirates they would steal the show. The whole point of giving stupid topics to the other classes was so that Class Six, her class, would appear wonderful. If only she had thought of letting Class Six be pirates. Pirates? It was monstrous!

By the time the end of the day arrived, Mrs Earwigger was still seething – she still hadn't come up with a plan that would put Miss Pandemonium in her place. The deputy head sent

the children home in a fit of bad temper –
not that they noticed, she seemed the same
as usual to them – and spent the whole
evening racking her brains for a solution.

4 Give Us Your Treasure!

A distant wail could be heard, rapidly approaching the school. 'It's Miss Pandemonium,' said Gary, and he was right. Violet's ambulance skidded into the car park and screeched to a halt. She jumped out, dropped half her bags, and skipped across the playground towards Class Five. The children watched from the windows.

'Do you think she's mad?' wondered Tina.

'I don't care,' Ryan said. 'She's changed The Earwig's plans, and I reckon she deserves a medal for bravery.'

The classroom door burst open and Miss Pandemonium rushed in, spilling the contents of one bag across the floor and

knocking six plants from their tray before
finally reaching her desk.

'Sorry I'm late,' she cried, 'but my
hamster got sucked up by the vacuum
cleaner. I switched to BLOW, and the poor
thing shot back out and landed in my bowl
of cornflakes. I had to take him to the
bathroom for a shampoo and blow-dry.
He's all right now, thank goodness, but I
think he's gone off cornflakes.'

'She *is* mad,' whispered Tracey to
Samantha.

'Is Michelle here yet?' asked Violet, smiling cheerfully at everyone.

'Over here, miss.'

'Did you get your uncle's monkey?' asked Miss Pandemonium.

'No, miss, he was out.' This was greeted by a roar from James.

'I said you didn't have a monkey. I said you wouldn't bring it in.'

'I do! I will! You see if I don't! I can't help it if my uncle was out.'

'Yeah? I bet you haven't even got an uncle, let alone a monkey.'

'James! Michelle!' cried Violet. 'I don't want to hear any more about it. The monkey isn't here today and that's fine. Perhaps you will be able to get hold of it for tomorrow, Michelle? It can join in the Fancy Dress fun.'

'I'll try, miss.'

Class Five settled down while Miss Pandemonium sorted out the register, and then they asked what they were going to do all day. Violet gazed at their expectant faces. 'Well, I thought we should spend the day getting into the spirit of being pirates, ready for tomorrow. You know what pirates used to do, don't you?'

'Kill people!' shouted Samantha Boggis. 'Can we kill Class Six, please, miss?'

'Not this week, Samantha, if you don't mind, and certainly not while I'm here. Pirates did a lot of kidnapping and marooning and holding people to ransom. They used to board ships and seize all their gold and jewels and then they'd sail off to secret islands and bury their ill-gotten gains.'

'Sounds good to me,' grinned Samantha.

'In my ambulance I have some bits and pieces that might be useful to us,' Miss Pandemonium went on. 'If we are going to turn this classroom into a pirate galleon we shall need swords and daggers, and cannons and cannon balls. We also need some treasure, and I thought we could make a few raids, like real pirates.'

Samantha Boggis could hardly believe her luck. 'Raids, miss? Real raids – I mean waving swords and threatening people and stealing all their treasure?'

'Not quite, Samantha. I think we shall leave out the threatening bit for a start. Where do you get your ideas from? I thought I'd send out a few children to go and raid the other classes, saying that they're pirates and demanding treasure. I'm sure the other teachers will join in the fun. After all, it is part of Book Week.'

'Then what do we do?' asked Tom.

'We bury it in a secret location; at least some of us bury it. I'm going to split the class into two teams. One team is going to bury the treasure, and then make a treasure map of the school to show where their treasure is buried. Then the other team will see if they can find it.'

Class Five gazed at Miss Pandemonium as if they were looking at an angel who worked miracles. 'That's brilliant,' breathed Neil. 'It will be fantastic.'

'What about The Earwig?' asked Tina. 'The Earwig won't like it at all.'

'The Earwig?' repeated Miss Pandemonium, with a tiny smile.

'Oh, sorry, miss.' Tina

turned bright red. 'I meant Mrs
Earwigger.'

'I would never have guessed. Don't
worry about Mrs Earwigger. I'm sure she'll
think it's all great fun. Now, come with me
and help get the stuff from the
ambulance.'

Most of the children spent the rest of the
morning hammering and sticking and
cutting and measuring and painting. But
the most fun was had by the raiders. For
some reason Miss Pandemonium decided
that Samantha Boggis wouldn't be a very
good raider, or perhaps it was that she
thought Samantha Boggis would be *too*
good. Instead she chose three children
who normally didn't get much of a look-in.

Ryan, Clyde and Linda were the
terrifying trio. They decided they would
start with easy pickings and they headed

straight for Mrs Patel's class of four- and five-year-olds. Outside Mrs Patel's classroom door the pirate raiders had a long argument about whether or not they should knock.

'It's stupid,' grumbled Clyde. 'Real pirates would never knock first.'

'But we're not actually real pirates, not really real, and you know what Mrs Earwigger does if you don't knock first.' Linda was nervously chewing her nails.

'Suppose we knock and then rush in quickly?' suggested Ryan.

But before they were able to do anything, the door opened and Mrs Patel stood there, smiling down at them. 'Hello, you three. Did you want something? You've been standing outside arguing for ages. We wondered what was going on, didn't we, children?'

Twenty-seven tiny faces turned and gazed at the three pirates standing by the door. Linda chewed her nails even more nervously. Ryan coughed and went red. Clyde summoned up all his courage.

'Please, miss, we're pirates,' he whispered, staring hard at the floor.

'What was that?' asked Mrs Patel, barely able to stop herself laughing out loud. Clyde clenched his fists.

'We're pirates!' he suddenly shouted,

with an immensely fierce scowl. 'And we've come to steal your treasure!'

'Yeah!' Ryan waved his pirate sword menacingly. Linda now had no nails left at all.

'Oh dear, children! I think we're being robbed by pirates!' Mrs Patel raised both arms in the air in surrender. 'You'd better come in,' she said, and led the way into the classroom. Mrs Patel went across to her desk and picked up an old biscuit tin, in which she kept emergency plasters and extra shoelaces and other useful things. 'This is my treasure tin,' she said. 'You can take this, but only if you leave us in peace.'

Clyde seized the tin. 'Thanks, Mrs Patel, that's great – I mean, yeah, and nobody move or the dame gets it!' He wasn't quite sure if pirates spoke like this or not, but at least it made him sound mean and dangerous. The pirates backed out of the room, pulled the door shut and raced off. They didn't stop till they were safely out of sight of Mrs Patel's classroom.

'Brilliant!' cried Ryan. 'We did it! We've got some treasure.'

'Can we go now?' whispered Linda.

'No way. We've got to get some more.' Clyde was already busy scheming. Flushed with the success of their first raid he grew bolder. 'Let's rob Mr Kuddle!'

Ryan's jaw dropped and Linda suddenly needed to go to the toilet, desperately. The boys stood and waited. Linda hoped that the raid would be over by the time she returned and was disappointed to find the boys still politely waiting for her.

The three pirates crept up to Mr Kuddle's office. This time even Clyde was sure that they ought to knock first, so he rapped loudly on the door and they burst in.

Mr Kuddle was half way through eating a cheese and tomato sandwich. He couldn't say much, at least not without quite a lot of cheese falling out of his mouth. 'Ah!' he managed.

'We're pirates!' cried Clyde. 'Give us all your treasure!'

'Please,' began Mr Kuddle, swallowing hard. 'Let's be friends. Call me Kevin . . .'

'Please, Kevin,' repeated Clyde. 'Give us all your treasure.'

'Right, ah, well, let's see.' Mr Kuddle began fishing in his pockets for loose change. He didn't seem to have quite the right idea. 'Are you collecting for charity? Which one is it?'

'We're pirates,' repeated Clyde, and he and Ryan waved their swords, while Linda

anxiously peered at Mr Kuddle over
Ryan's shoulder.

'Of course – you're from Miss
Pandemonium's class, aren't you?' smiled
Mr Kuddle.

'We're from Captain Blackbeard's pirate
galleon!' corrected Clyde. 'And if you don't

hand over some treasure quick, I'll slice your ears off!'

'Ooooh!' squeaked Linda, and hurried back to the toilet.

Mr Kuddle looked suitably horrified and, after a quick glance round his room, handed over the little silver trophy that the football team had won that spring. 'Please don't slice my ears off,' he pleaded.

'We won't,' snarled Ryan. 'Not this time . . . Kevin.'

The Class Five raiders made one more swoop, this time on Miss Goodly, who immediately offered to hand over her entire class to the pirates because, she said, her children were all 'little treasures'.

Clyde didn't have an answer to this, but Ryan threatened to tie her up and make her walk the gangplank unless she gave them some proper treasure. Miss Goodly quickly gave them a box of giant pearls disguised as marbles, and the two boys returned to their classroom triumphant.

'Where's Linda?' asked Miss Pandemonium. 'I hope she hasn't been captured.'

'No, she went to the toilet, miss,' explained Clyde, and the class set about sorting through the treasure, ready for burying.

5 Tricky Tracey

Miss Pandemonium thought it would be a good idea if the treasure was hidden straight after lunch. Samantha Boggis led the burying party and, having threatened the other team with instant death if they tried to spy on her, she set off with her pirates to bury their treasure.

'Where are we going?' asked Mike.

'Somewhere the others will never think of looking, never dare to look.'

'Such as?'

'Shut up, I'll have to think.' They peered into the hall, but Mrs Earwigger was in there taking a PE lesson with Class Six. The children watched in fascination as eleven totally silent children climbed up ropes, balanced on benches and did forward rolls on the mats.

'How does she get them so quiet?' whispered Cleo. 'It's not natural.'

'And what's happened to the rest of the class?' asked Mike.

Samantha simply pointed to the far end of the hall. A long line of twenty-one children stood silently facing the wall, with their hands on their heads.

At that moment, Mrs Earwigger gave a

shrill cry and another child joined the wall-watchers. 'By the time The Earwig has taken PE for ten minutes the whole class will be standing there,' muttered Samantha. 'Come on, there's no time to lose. I've just had a brilliant idea.'

'What? What is it?' The treasure buriers hurried after their leader, all wanting to know what she was up to. She grinned back over her shoulder at them and stopped outside Class Six.

'We're going to bury our treasure here – in The Earwig's classroom. The others may discover where it's hidden, but they'll never dare try and get it while The Earwig's in there!'

Samantha was perfectly correct in her thinking. Nobody in their right mind would go into The Earwig's class while she was there.

'Cleo, Mike – you keep a look out.'

Clutching the treasure chest, Samantha and her horde hurried into Class Six and gazed round for a suitable hiding place. There were neat piles of clothes on the desks, which the children had changed out of for PE.

'They've folded their clothes!' Tom couldn't believe his eyes. 'Every single thing – even their socks! That is weird, and I mean weird!'

'Everyone goes weird in here,' said Ravi, making it sound as if you might well catch the plague or yellow fever.

Samantha's gaze fell upon the big cupboard in the corner. Inside were tins of paint, paper, pencils, rulers, books, scissors – all sorts. She stretched up as high as she could manage and, with an enormously satisfied grin, pushed the chest on to the top shelf. There was a scuffle at the door.

'Earwig's coming!' hissed Mike. 'Scram!'

The children just had time to shut the cupboard door and slip out of the room before Mrs Earwigger appeared, followed by a neat line of girls and a neat line of boys – all silent. From their hiding place in the cloakroom, Samantha and her gang watched Class Six file into their classroom. The door closed.

'Brilliant!' she chuckled. 'I can't wait!

Let's get back to the classroom and draw the map.'

The treasure seekers were under the command of Darren and Tracey, and they set off at great speed and with high hopes. Tom Nunnery had drawn the treasure map, and he had tried to make it look as authentic as possible. Mrs Patel's classroom had 'Here be tiny people' written across it, while Mr Kuddle's office was called 'Cave of the Big Chief'. Above Class Six it said 'Beware of the Dragon', and there was a big black cross showing that the treasure was buried in the corner of the cave.

The treasure seekers were not terribly good at map-reading, and it took them quite a while to get their bearings and work out what Tom's strange clues meant. They walked round the hall four times.

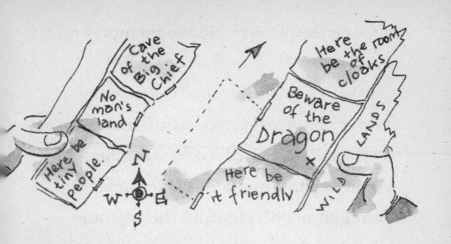

'Trouble is,' muttered Tracey, 'you can't tell which way round this map goes. Who are the little people, anyway? I reckon Samantha's just playing tricks on us.'

It was Gary who solved the problem. 'It says there's a dragon, and there's only one dragon in this school that I know of, and that's The Earwig.' They hurried down the corridor until they neared Class Six. Darren studied the map carefully.

'Yeah, look, if Class Six is where the dragon is, then Mrs Patel's would be where the little people are – all the infants, see? Excellent!'

'I don't know what you're so pleased about,' said Tracey. 'According to this map the treasure is buried inside Class Six.'

The children could not hide their disappointment. 'How did they get it in there?' demanded Ryan, but nobody knew. 'Well, if someone got it in there then someone must be able to get it out again,' said Ryan. 'We need a plan.' The children began thinking hard.

'We need to know exactly where the treasure is buried,' declared Tracey. 'Look, it's in this corner, on the map. What's in the corner of the classroom? Tony, you take a look.'

'Me? How?'

'Just take a quick peek through the window in the door, stupid.'

'Supposing I'm spotted?'

'You'll be **OK**, go on.' Darren gave Tony a shove and Tony suddenly found himself crouching outside Mrs Earwigger's door.

Very, very slowly he inched his way upwards, until his eyes were just peeping over the bottom frame of the window. He peered into Class Six, and met the icy glare of the deputy head on full red alert.

'That boy there!' The Earwig's voice could be heard even in the cloakroom where the other treasure seekers were now crouching, holding their breath. The door crashed open and Mrs Earwigger fixed

Tony with her freezing eyes. 'What do you think you are doing, Tony Williams?'

Poor Tony squeezed his eyes up tight and tried ever so hard to think of a good answer, but none came. 'I don't know, Mrs Earwigger,' he whispered.

'You don't know? I see. Did Miss Pandemonium send you?'

'Um, yes, no, yes, I mean – no.'

The deputy head grabbed Tony's shoulder in a grip of iron. 'You can stand up against the wall in my classroom until you think of a sensible answer. Go on!' Tony vanished inside and the door slammed.

'That worked really well, Tracey,' said Darren.

'Excuse me,' said Tracey. 'Do you have any better ideas? Anyhow, I saw a big cupboard in the corner when Mrs

Earwigger opened the door. I bet they've hidden the treasure chest in the cupboard. How can we get the Earwig out of the classroom, so that we can get inside?'

'Give her a message,' said Gary. 'Tell her Mr Kuddle needs to see her, or something.' The treasure seekers looked at Gary. This was about the third good idea he'd had in two days. Obviously he was a lot cleverer than they gave him credit for.

'Excellent idea,' said Tracey. 'OK, a message – how about "Mr Kuddle says there is an important telephone message for you"? Then she'll have to go all the way down to the office and back again. That's plenty of time. Let's go!'

The others stared at

her. 'Your idea,' they said. 'You do it.'

Tracey mumbled a few dark threats but she knew she didn't have much choice. She took a deep breath and approached the dragon's lair.

Outside the door she stopped and glanced back at the cloakroom. 'Go on!' hissed Darren and Gary. Tracey swallowed hard and knocked. She heard footsteps clicking towards the door. The handle rattled. The door opened, and Tracey's heart stopped.

'Yes? What is it now?'

'Please, Mrs Earwigger, Mr Kuddle says that there is an important telephone message for you.'

'Really? Why did he send you? Why didn't he come himself?'

'I – I don't know,' stammered Tracey, 'I was with the secretary and the phone rang and then he came in and saw me and sent me up here to you.' Tracey was astonished at her own boldness. The deputy head glanced back at her class.

'Not a word while I'm out of the room,' she ordered. 'Get on with your maths.'

Mrs Earwigger strode off down the corridor. The moment the deputy had disappeared round the corner the treasure seekers dashed out from the cloakroom and raced into her classroom. As they poured in through the door they suddenly realized that they had not taken into account one small problem. They had got rid of Mrs Earwigger, but they hadn't got rid of Mrs Earwigger's class. Year Six glared at them menacingly. 'What do you lot want?' demanded John. Once again Tracey's brain started working overtime.

'Us? Miss Pandemonium sent us to fetch

something. She said it was in this cupboard.' Tracey smiled and stepped towards the cupboard. John slowly got to his feet, and so did several other class members.

'Oh really? What was it?'

'Paint,' said Tracey, pulling open a door and spotting several tins of the stuff on the shelves. 'She said she'd run out of Leaf Green.' Tracey's quick eye also saw the treasure chest on the top shelf, and she winked at the others. Class Six were very suspicious. They didn't seem to believe Tracey at all. 'Oh look!' she suddenly cried, pointing out through the classroom window, and as Class Six turned away she put a foot on the bottom shelf and heaved herself up towards the treasure.

'What?' growled John, gazing out of the window.

'A bird, I saw a bird – big – a huge bird, an ostrich probably . . .' Tracey's voice was rather muffled by the cupboard and John turned back to see what was going on.

'Oi! Get down! You can't do that! cried John, and he threw himself towards the cupboard and tried to wrench Tracey away. Half of Class Six plunged after him, while the small gang of treasure seekers desperately tried to make their escape.

Tracey clung to the top shelf, but as John pulled harder and harder at her legs

the whole cupboard
began to topple
forward. Paper,
pencils and tins
of paint slid
from the
shelves and
cascaded
down on to
the floor.
Suddenly,
Tracey let go with a
yell and the cupboard rocked back into
place. But the damage was done. Paint tins
crashed to the floor and their lids pinged
off, scattering powder colours everywhere.
Sheets of paper were strewn far and wide.
Tracey and the gang fought to escape, but
the more they fought the more Class Six
piled on top of them and the more things

flew about the room. A rainbow-coloured cloud of paint powder swirled up into the air.

And then a huge, black vulture swept into the room. Mrs Earwigger had returned.

6 Mrs Earwigger's Revenge

Even above the shrieks and screams of the multicoloured children, Mrs Earwigger's whistle could be heard. The squirming pile stopped wriggling and a deathly silence fell across the classroom. Terrified faces peered up at her. The deputy head stood in the doorway with her eyes on stalks and her beehive hairdo quivering with a mixture of rage and horror.

'What is going on?' she hissed and immediately held up both hands. 'No – I don't want to hear a word of excuse, nothing. This behaviour is intolerable. Tracey Perkins, Darren Wellbrook – I take it that is you underneath all that paint powder – you're not even in my class.

What's been going on? No – don't tell me
– out to the hall, all of you – and my class
too. Go on, hands on heads, walking – go
and stand in the hall while I fetch Mr
Kuddle and Miss Pandemonium. We'll
soon get to the bottom of this and then
there'll be trouble. If you think any of you
have seen me at my worst then you are in
for a very nasty shock! Go on – move!'

Thirty paint-spattered children
trailed into the hall and lined up along
the wall. The double doors banged

and back came Mrs Earwigger, her face like a hurricane, dragging a bemused Mr Kuddle and Miss Pandemonium in her wake.

The inquisition began, and Mrs Earwigger soon discovered the cause of the chaos.

'This is absolutely appalling,' declared the deputy. 'Are you telling me that some children from Class Five hid treasure in my cupboard, and that these silly children here tried to sneak in and get it back?' Tracey, Darren and the rest of the treasure seekers shuffled their feet and nodded glumly. 'Mr Kuddle, can you believe such a thing?'

The head teacher didn't appear quite so horrified as his deputy. 'Well, actually, it sounds rather fun to me.'

'Fun? FUN?!?'

'Yes. I think it was rather a clever place to hide the treasure. After all, nobody would dare go into your classroom normally . . . if you see what I mean . . .' Mr Kuddle swallowed hard as he felt Mrs Earwigger's eyes upon him.

'It was a harmless bit of fun for Book Week,' explained Miss Pandemonium. 'It got out of hand, that's all. If the children from your class hadn't tried to stop the treasure seekers everything would be all right.'

Mrs Earwigger turned her flame-thrower eyes upon Miss Pandemonium. It was a wonder her glasses didn't melt from the heat. 'Did you know about this?'

'But of course, it was my idea.' Violet looked straight back at Mrs Earwigger with her flame-proof grey eyes. 'We made a treasure chest, hid it and then drew a map to show where it was. The treasure seekers had to find it and bring it back.'

'Fascinating,' murmured Mr Kuddle.

'Is that what schools do now?' cried Mrs Earwigger bitterly. 'Is that meant to be education?'

Miss Pandemonium remained calm. 'It involved grids, use of map keys, interpretation, logic, language, communication skills, team-work and personal initiative.' Put like this, it sounded as if the children had just completed the Duke of Edinburgh Award Scheme. 'It was clever of Tracey to think of a way to get you to leave your classroom.' Miss Pandemonium gave the deputy a broad smile. 'You must admit, Mrs Earwigger, that it has been rather fun.'

'Fun?!?' exploded the deputy yet again. 'My classroom is a rubbish tip!'

'The treasure seekers can help clear up your room, Mrs Earwigger. Now, if you'll excuse me I must get back to the rest of my pirates.'

Miss Pandemonium trotted off across the hall and disappeared back to her classroom. Outside her door Tony Williams was waiting for her. He had an enormous grin right across his face and was clutching a big box. 'Look, miss – I got the treasure chest!'

'Tony! Well done. How on earth did you manage that?'

'Well, when Mrs Earwigger started fuming and frothing she sent all the children out to the hall, but she forgot all about me because I was still standing in the corner at the back. So I just went to the cupboard and got the treasure chest.'

'Brilliant! What a wonderful day we've had. It's almost home-time, so clear everything away. Don't forget it's Dressing-up Day tomorrow. I want to see thirty wonderful pirates. If today was a good day, then tomorrow is going to be fantabu-wonderlasticallytremendiddlyendous!'

The following morning, Witts End Primary School looked totally different. A crowd of excited children sat in the hall, waiting for assembly, wearing costumes of all kinds, sizes and colours. Michelle had even brought her uncle's monkey at last, although it wasn't a real one. It was a rather tattered cloth monkey, with one ear missing. Michelle's uncle still went to sleep with it at night.

The only person not in fancy dress was Mrs Earwigger, but instead of wearing a costume the deputy head was wearing something far more unexpected and astonishing – a smile.

'Nice to see her looking cheerful for once,' the secretary said to Snow White, alias Mrs Patel.

'Yes, I wonder what she's been up to.'

Mr Kuddle entered the hall and assembly began. He was dressed up himself, as Widow Twankey, although his bushy moustache was a bit of a give-away. He told the children about the timetable

for the day. 'As you know, it is our Library
Opening Day today, and the Mayor has
kindly agreed to come along and perform
the opening ceremony. I am sure he will be
delighted to see such a wonderful display
of fancy dress. Don't forget that there will
be prizes for the best costumes. The
newspapers are coming too and they will

be taking photographs. It is going to be a very exciting morning, so remember to behave well in front of our distinguished visitors and . . .'

At that moment the double doors at the rear of the hall burst open and Mrs Earwigger hurried in. She was waving both her arms frantically at Widow Twankey, and Mr Kuddle's voice trailed away. The deputy head hurried up the length of the hall

and then began a long, whispered conversation with Mr Kuddle. He frowned, groaned and raised his eyes heavenwards in complete dismay. Then he turned and faced the children.

'I'm very sorry,' he began. 'There has been a bit of a mix-up. Mrs Earwigger says the secretary has just received a telephone call from the Town Hall to say that the Mayor cannot come today because of more important commitments. He's sorry, but he won't be able to open the new library after all.'

The disappointment among the children was huge. A groan went up that would have made the hardest heart weep. Poor Mr Kuddle struggled to think of something that might help to save the situation. He raised a hand for some quiet.

'Don't forget that we still have our lovely

costumes, and the press will still be coming to take photograaa . . .'

Mrs Earwigger whispered into the head's ear once again, and he turned away in despair. This time it was the deputy who spoke to the hall. 'Since the Mayor is unable to come there really is no point in the press coming to take pictures, so I telephoned the newspaper offices and cancelled their visit. I am very much afraid, children, that nobody is coming here today at all.'

Violet Pandemonium was watching Mrs Earwigger very carefully, and wondering why the deputy head seemed somehow pleased. Although Mrs Earwigger was looking at the children very seriously, there was something about her that made Violet think she was just acting. Very quietly, she slipped from her chair and hurried down the empty corridor to the secretary's office.

'Isn't it awful,' said the secretary. 'The children must be so disappointed. I couldn't believe it when Mrs Earwigger came in and told me that the Mayor had cancelled and she had to cancel the newspapers.'

Miss Pandemonium took a deep breath. Everything was beginning to make sense. 'I thought the Mayor had rung you?' she said to the secretary.

'Oh no.'

'Quick, ring the Town Hall! There's something fishy going on.'

The secretary hastily dialled the Town Hall and Miss Pandemonium seized the phone and began firing questions at the poor official at the other end. After several minutes, Violet slammed the phone back down. 'Mrs Earwigger has made the whole thing up. She rang the Town Hall late yesterday and said that we had to cancel. Now the Mayor has gone off shopping for some new trousers. Mrs Earwigger has made the whole thing up!'

'How could she? I mean, why? What shall we do? The poor children . . .' moaned the secretary, but Miss Pandemonium was not going to be defeated.

'You telephone the press and get them back here on the double. I shall sort out the Mayor!'

Miss Pandemonium raced back up the

corridor and burst into the hall, which was still a scene of doom and gloom. 'Excuse me, Mr Kuddle,' cried Violet. 'Small emergency – must dash – I shall be back very shortly – keep the children in the hall – Samantha, Gary, Mike, Laura, Ravi, Kimberley, you come with me, quick, on the double, come on, and bring your swords!' And with that Miss Pandemonium and her pirate gang hurried out to her ambulance. A few moments later, with siren blaring and lights flashing, the ambulance was screaming towards the centre of town.

7 The Pirates Go Kidnapping

'Where are we going, miss?' asked Ravi, as the ambulance tore up the High Street.

'Just keep your eyes open for the Mayor,' Miss Pandemonium answered grimly.

'There's his car!' Laura shouted suddenly. 'Look, with the little flag on the front.'

Miss Pandemonium brought the ambulance to a screeching halt behind the Mayor's big black limousine. 'Come on, he must be in the shop. We've got to get him back to school as quickly as possible. Raiding party – are you ready?'

'Ready, miss!'

'OK – follow me!'

Waving their wooden swords ferociously,

the pirate gang piled out of the ambulance and burst into the department store, much to the surprise and horror of the customers. 'He'll be in the Menswear bit!' cried Violet, and promptly went dashing up the down escalator the wrong way. The smaller pirates followed on the proper escalator and were at the top long before Violet arrived, puffing and panting.

Safe in his office, the store manager was on the telephone to the police. 'Yes,' he hissed. 'It's a raid! They're disguised as pirates. Quick – for heaven's sake get up here at once!'

Up in the Menswear Department the Mayor had found a rather nice pair of trousers and had wandered off to the changing room to try them on.

'There he goes!' pointed Kimberley. 'Over there, miss!'

'Come on!' yelled Samantha and without further ado she dashed across to the changing rooms. As the seven pirates launched their ambush, panic broke out. Several men came running out of the changing rooms clutching half-undone trousers and shirts. The poor Mayor had only just taken off his old pair of trousers when he was set upon by the pirates, whisked off his feet, and carried away, shouting for help and waving his hairy legs in mid-air.

'I want my trousers back! This is outrageous! I am the Mayor – put me down!'

'Quieten down, you scum!' roared Samantha in her fiercest pirate voice, 'or I'll cut off your ears!'

'Ooooh,' squeaked the Mayor, and he went deathly quiet at once.

Several staff and customers tried to
come to the Mayor's rescue, rushing upon
the kidnappers and attacking them with an
array of coat hangers, hat stands,
umbrellas and handbags. The pirates,
though, had had far more practice in the
school playground and easily kept their
attackers at bay.

Once outside, they bundled the Mayor
into the ambulance. Miss Pandemonium

took off at once, with a squeal of burning rubber and clouds of smoke, closely followed by two wailing police cars, which had just arrived on the scene.

'This is brilliant!' said Gary, leaning out of the window. 'I like being a pirate.'

By the time the ambulance reached the school, the Mayor had managed to get his trousers back on and Miss Pandemonium had explained just what had been going on, and how Mrs Earwigger had tried to trick them all. 'I'm sorry,' she said, 'but there was no time to lose. I knew we just had to get you here as quickly as possible. Everyone is still at school, all dressed up and waiting for you to open the library.'

The Mayor sat next to her in the front, gripping the edge of his seat for safety as Violet flung the ambulance round a corner on two wheels. He gave her a pale, but excited smile. 'It's great fun,' he chuckled. 'I haven't enjoyed myself so much for ages. Fancy being kidnapped by ten-year-old pirates! I wish all library-openings were like this! It's going to make a wonderful newspaper story. Quick, turn left down this alley, it's a short cut.'

Screeching into the car park, the ambulance had hardly come to a halt before everyone leapt out and went charging into school. Miss Pandemonium led the way. 'Leave the talking to me,' she hissed as they marched into the hall. A sea of expectant little faces watched.

'What's going on!' cried Mrs Earwigger. Violet gave her a little smile.

'It's quite all right, Mrs Earwigger. There has been a little bit of a mix-up. Allow me to introduce the Mayor. He has come to open the library after all.'

'But that's impossible!' spluttered the deputy. 'I shan't allow it.' Then, as if to add strength to Mrs Earwigger's words, the double doors burst open and four policemen charged into the hall.

'Hold it right there!' yelled Inspector Hole.

Mr Kuddle, or rather Widow Twankey, stepped forward with a remarkably cheerful smile. 'What – more fancy dress?' he began. 'Isn't that nice, children? The newspaper reporters have dressed up too.'

'I'm not a reporter, I'm a real policeman!' screamed Inspector Hole, 'and you are under arrest for kidnapping, assault, speeding and and and . . .'

Inspector Hole suddenly stopped and eyed Mr Kuddle with undisguised horror.

'You're the headmaster! You've got a moustache!'

'That's right.'

'You're wearing a dress!'

'Yes. Can I have a go on your whistle?'

'No, stop it, put my whistle down. Arrest those pirates!'

The policemen waded in among the children and were about to arrest the pirates when the Mayor came to the rescue. He hastily explained to the inspector that he was at the school to open the library, that it was Dressing-up Day, and so on. Calm began to descend. Only Mrs Earwigger was becoming more and more worked up as she realized her plan was about to fail.

Just as the deputy was going into her mouth-disappearing act and getting ready to have a minor explosion, a rescue party arrived in the shape of the real reporter and photographer. As soon as the deputy head saw the press cameras, her whole attitude changed and her face beamed a bright smile. She simpered ever so sweetly, patted her hair into place and hurried across the hall. 'Ah, dear gentlemen of the press – you've come to photograph Class Six of course!'

'Well, actually, we haven't decided what . . .'

'Of course you want my class,' insisted Mrs Earwigger. 'And me too. We are by far the best dressed. Besides, we are the eldest. Come on, my class, on your feet.'

As Class Six got to their feet the other teachers and children looked desperately at each other. One moment Mrs Earwigger was trying to ruin the show and the next she was hogging the limelight. All eyes turned to Miss Pandemonium. Surely Miss Pandemonium could stop this outrage? But it wasn't Violet who came to the rescue at all, it was Widow Twankey.

'I think the Music Room would be the

best place for a photograph, Mrs
Earwigger,' said Mr Kuddle. 'It's nice
and quiet in there and the press can take
as much time as they want. Follow me,
Class Six.' The head teacher led the
children out of the room. When they
reached the Music Room door Mr
Kuddle turned to Mrs Earwigger. 'You'd
better go in and check that it's clear,' he
suggested.

'I must say this is a very good idea of
yours, Mr Kuddle,' said the deputy,
marching into the Music Room. 'At least
my class won't be disturbed by those
horrible pirates.'

No sooner was she inside than Mr
Kuddle pulled the door shut and locked it.
'Now,' he said calmly, 'let's all go back to
the hall and do what we want to do for a
change.' He led the children back to the

hall, ignoring the muffled cries from inside the sound-proofed Music Room.

After that, the library opening ceremony went very well indeed. The Mayor made a funny speech, invited all the policemen in, and everyone ate cake. The press took so many photographs the school ended up with a double-page spread in the newspaper.

It was all rather enjoyable, but what everyone noticed most of all was how relaxing it was, how jolly everyone felt, how helpful and thoughtful everyone was, now that Mrs Earwigger was shut in the Music Room. 'I suppose someone ought to let her out,' said Mrs Patel.

'I've lost the key,' snapped Widow Twankey. After years of putting up with Mrs Earwigger, Mr Kuddle wasn't going to let her off that easily.

'I'll save her a piece of cake,' said Miss Pandemonium quietly.

As it happened, Mrs Earwigger would have found it difficult to come out even if she had wanted to. Stuck inside the Music Room, she had become desperate to escape, but apart from the locked door the only way out was through a window in the flat roof which was too high for her to reach.

Looking around, Mrs Earwigger noticed a pile of drums. There were four altogether, starting with a little snarc drum and going up to the big bass drum. The deputy reckoned that if she put one drum on top of the other she could climb up, stand on the top and reach the window – and freedom.

Making the drum-mountain was easy. Climbing up the mountain with her dress hitched up round her knees was a bit more difficult. Balancing on the top of the wobbly mountain while trying to open a window was very difficult indeed. The pile began to quiver and quake, with Mrs Earwigger frantically dancing about on the

summit, trying to stay upright –
unsuccessfully.

'Aaaaaaargh!'

With a thunderous crash Mrs
Earwigger's feet disappeared through the
top drum. Then her whole body came
crashing after her feet, pushing her down
inside all four drums, pinning her arms to
her sides and leaving her barely able to
move.

And that was how they found her at
half-past three after the children had gone
home. Mr Kuddle, who by this time had
changed back into his normal clothes,
found the key and unlocked the Music
Room door. He peered inside. 'Well, it
looks as if Mrs Earwigger has decided to
come in fancy dress after all.'

From between the top two drums a tiny
chink allowed Mrs Earwigger to peer out

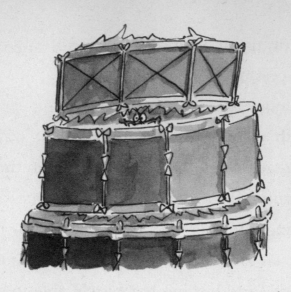

helplessly. 'Out of my way!' she hissed
furiously.

'Would you like some help to get out of
those drums?' Miss Goodly asked.

'Just get out of my way!' cried the
deputy once again and the mountain of
drums began to slowly shuffle across the
floor towards them. In astonished silence
the staff stood back and watched as the
drum-pile set off along the corridor and
headed home.

Mr Kuddle watched her go and smiled cheerfully. Somehow he reckoned that when Mrs Earwigger returned to the school – if she returned – she would not be nearly so troublesome. And if she was, well, he could always call on Violet Pandemonium to come and sort things out.

Jeremy Strong

The Desperate Adventures of Sir Rupert and Rosie Gusset

'It's so exciting!' Rosie cried. 'Just think, Father, all those adventures! Fighting Mad Mavis! Looking for treasure!'

Just the thought of setting sail makes Sir Rupert feel seasick. And the possibility of bumping into his rival, Sir Sidney Dribble, or Mad Mavis and her pirate gang, makes him feel even worse. Luckily Sir Rupert's daughter, Rosie, isn't quite such a wimp as he is.

Jeremy Strong

My Dad's Got an Alligator

'It's that alligator ... Dad should never have brought it into the house. Crunchbag has escaped and he's eaten Granny!'

When Nicholas's dad brings an alligator home, the family thinks he has finally flipped. Crunchbag is soon running riot: in the bath, on the roof-rack and on the loose! It seems there's no mischief he won't get up to. But can he really have eaten Granny?

Jeremy Strong

The Hundred-Mile-An-Hour Dog

WHOOSH!
Is it a bird? Is it a plane?
No, it's the hundred-mile-an-hour dog!

Streaker is no ordinary dog. She's a rocket on four legs with a woof attached, and Trevor has got until the end of the holidays to train her. If he fails, he'll lose his bet with horrible Charlie Smugg, and something very nasty to do with frogspawn will happen.

Jeremy Strong

The Indoor Pirates

A hopelessly silly piratical adventure.

Captain Blackpatch has always hated the sea – even though he's a pirate. So when he inherits No. 25 Dolphin Street, he moves in and invites his friends Lumpy Lawson, Bald Ben, and the twins Polly and Molly to join him. They make the house look as much like a ship as possible and practise very hard at being piratical, but the bills are mounting up and there's not a treasure chest in sight. Unluckily, Captain Blackpatch has a plan …

Jeremy Strong

Viking at School

Tim grinned at his classmates, and they stared back at the great big, hairy Viking sitting in their classroom

Sigurd the Viking is back in Flotby, but not everyone is pleased to see him. Mr and Mrs Ellis don t know what to do with him until they hit upon a brilliant idea perhaps a short spell at school would teach the Viking some twenti-eth-century manners ...

READ MORE IN PUFFIN

For children of all ages, Puffin represents quality and variety – the very best in publishing today around the world.

For complete information about books available from Puffin – and Penguin – and how to order them, contact us at the appropriate address below. Please note that for copyright reasons the selection of books varies from country to country.

On the worldwide web: www.puffin.co.uk

In the United Kingdom: Please write to *Dept. EP, Penguin Books Ltd, Bath Road, Harmondsworth, West Drayton, Middlesex UB7 ODA*

In the United States: Please write to *Consumer Sales, Penguin USA, P.O. Box 999, Dept. 17109, Bergenfield, New Jersey 07621-0120.* VISA and MasterCard holders call 1-800-253-6476 to order Penguin titles

In Canada: Please write to *Penguin Books Canada Ltd, 10 Alcorn Avenue, Suite 300, Toronto, Ontario M4V 3B2*

In Australia: Please write to *Penguin Books Australia Ltd, P.O. Box 257, Ringwood, Victoria 3134*

In New Zealand: Please write to *Penguin Books (NZ) Ltd, Private Bag 102902, North Shore Mail Centre, Auckland 10*

In India: Please write to *Penguin Books India Pvt Ltd, 706 Eros Apartments, 56 Nehru Place, New Delhi 110 019*

In the Netherlands: Please write to *Penguin Books Netherlands bv, Postbus 3507, NL-1001 AH Amsterdam*

In Germany: Please write to *Penguin Books Deutschland GmbH, Metzlerstrasse 26, 60594 Frankfurt am Main*

In Spain: Please write to *Penguin Books S. A., Bravo Murillo 19, 1° B, 28015 Madrid*

In Italy: Please write to *Penguin Italia s.r.l., Via Felice Casati 20, I–20124 Milano*

In France: Please write to *Penguin France S. A., 17 rue Lejeune, F–31000 Toulouse*

In Japan: Please write to *Penguin Books Japan, Ishikiribashi Building, 2–5–4, Suido, Bunkyo-ku, Tokyo 112*

In South Africa: Please write to *Longman Penguin Southern Africa (Pty) Ltd, Private Bag X08, Bertsham 2013*